Soccer on Sunday

Magic Tree House® Books

#1: DINOSAURS BEFORE DARK
#2: THE KNIGHT AT DAWN
#3: MUMMIES IN THE MORNING
#4: PIRATES PAST NOON
#5: NIGHT OF THE NINJAS
#6: AFTERNOON ON THE AMAZON
#7: SUNSET OF THE SABERTOOTH
#8: MIDNIGHT ON THE MOON
#9: DOLPHINS AT DAYBREAK
#10: GHOST TOWN AT SUNDOWN
#11: LIONS AT LUNCHTIME
#12: POLAR BEARS PAST BEDTIME
#13: VACATION UNDER THE VOLCANO
#14: DAY OF THE DRAGON KING
#15: VIKING SHIPS AT SUNRISE
#16: HOUR OF THE OLYMPICS
#17: TONIGHT ON THE *TITANIC*
#18: BUFFALO BEFORE BREAKFAST
#19: TIGERS AT TWILIGHT
#20: DINGOES AT DINNERTIME
#21: CIVIL WAR ON SUNDAY
#22: REVOLUTIONARY WAR
ON WEDNESDAY
#23: TWISTER ON TUESDAY
#24: EARTHQUAKE IN THE
EARLY MORNING
#25: STAGE FRIGHT ON A
SUMMER NIGHT
#26: GOOD MORNING, GORILLAS
#27: THANKSGIVING ON THURSDAY
#28: HIGH TIDE IN HAWAII

Merlin Missions

#29: CHRISTMAS IN CAMELOT
#30: HAUNTED CASTLE ON HALLOWS EVE
#31: SUMMER OF THE SEA SERPENT
#32: WINTER OF THE ICE WIZARD
#33: CARNIVAL AT CANDLELIGHT
#34: SEASON OF THE SANDSTORMS
#35: NIGHT OF THE NEW MAGICIANS
#36: BLIZZARD OF THE BLUE MOON
#37: DRAGON OF THE RED DAWN
#38: MONDAY WITH A MAD GENIUS
#39: DARK DAY IN THE DEEP SEA
#40: EVE OF THE EMPEROR PENGUIN
#41: MOONLIGHT ON THE MAGIC FLUTE
#42: A GOOD NIGHT FOR GHOSTS

#43: LEPRECHAUN IN LATE WINTER
#44: A GHOST TALE FOR CHRISTMAS TIME
#45: A CRAZY DAY WITH COBRAS
#46: DOGS IN THE DEAD OF NIGHT
#47: ABE LINCOLN AT LAST!
#48: A PERFECT TIME FOR PANDAS
#49: STALLION BY STARLIGHT
#50: HURRY UP, HOUDINI!
#51: HIGH TIME FOR HEROES

Magic Tree House® Fact Trackers

DINOSAURS
KNIGHTS AND CASTLES
MUMMIES AND PYRAMIDS
PIRATES
RAIN FORESTS
SPACE
TITANIC
TWISTERS AND OTHER TERRIBLE STORMS
DOLPHINS AND SHARKS
ANCIENT GREECE AND THE OLYMPICS
AMERICAN REVOLUTION
SABERTOOTHS AND THE ICE AGE
PILGRIMS
ANCIENT ROME AND POMPEII
TSUNAMIS AND OTHER NATURAL DISASTERS
POLAR BEARS AND THE ARCTIC
SEA MONSTERS
PENGUINS AND ANTARCTICA
LEONARDO DA VINCI
GHOSTS
LEPRECHAUNS AND IRISH FOLKLORE
RAGS AND RICHES: KIDS IN THE TIME OF
CHARLES DICKENS
SNAKES AND OTHER REPTILES
DOG HEROES
ABRAHAM LINCOLN
PANDAS AND OTHER ENDANGERED SPECIES
HORSE HEROES
HEROES FOR ALL TIMES
 SOCCER

More Magic Tree House®

GAMES AND PUZZLES FROM THE TREE HOUSE
MAGIC TRICKS FROM THE TREE HOUSE
MY MAGIC TREE HOUSE JOURNAL

MAGIC TREE HOUSE® #52
A MERLIN MISSION

Soccer on Sunday

by Mary Pope Osborne

illustrated by Sal Murdocca

A STEPPING STONE BOOK™

Random House 🏠 New York

Visit us on the Web!
randomhouse.com/kids
MagicTreeHouse.com

Educators and librarians, for a variety of teaching tools, visit us at
RHTeachersLibrarians.com

Library of Congress Cataloging-in-Publication Data
Osborne, Mary Pope.
Soccer on Sunday / by Mary Pope Osborne ; illustrated by Sal Murdocca.
pages cm. — (Magic tree house ; #52)
Summary: "Jack and Annie search for the fourth secret of greatness for Merlin the Magician in Mexico City at the 1970 World Cup Games. They hope to learn something new from soccer player great, Pele." —Provided by publisher.
ISBN 978-0-307-98053-3 (trade) — ISBN 978-0-307-98054-0 (lib. bdg.) — ISBN 978-0-307-98055-7 (ebook)
[1. Magic—Fiction. 2. Time travel—Fiction. 3. Brothers and sisters—Fiction. 4. Soccer—Fiction. 5. Pelé, 1940—Fiction. 6. Mexico—History—1946–1970—Fiction.] I. Murdocca, Sal, illustrator. II. Title.
PZ7.O81167 Sl 2014 [Fic]—dc23 2013042092

Printed in the United States of America
10 9 8 7 6 5 4 3 2 1
First Edition

To Malcolm Edson Nascimento DeLuca,
grandson of Pelé the Great

CONTENTS

Prologue

One summer day in Frog Creek, Pennsylvania, a mysterious tree house appeared in the woods. It was filled with books. A boy named Jack and his sister, Annie, found the tree house and soon discovered that it was magic. They could go to any time and place in history just by pointing to a picture in one of the books. While they were gone, no time at all passed back in Frog Creek.

Jack and Annie eventually found out that the tree house belonged to Morgan le Fay, a magical librarian from the legendary realm of Camelot. They have since traveled on many adventures in the magic tree house and completed many missions for both Morgan le Fay and her friend Merlin the magician.

Now Merlin needs Jack and Annie's help again. He wants them to travel through time and learn secrets of greatness from four people who are called great by the world. Jack and Annie have completed three of the four missions. They took a trip to ancient Macedonia, where they spent time with Alexander the Great and his war-horse, Bucephalus; they visited Coney Island in 1908, where they saw Harry Houdini and his wife, Bess, perform a magic show; and they had an adventure in Egypt in the 1800s, where they met Florence Nightingale.

Back in Frog Creek, they are waiting to see where Merlin will send them to find the fourth secret of greatness. . . .

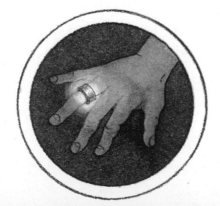

ONE

Seriously?

Slowly and carefully, Jack ran his hands over the face of the stony cliff. His fingers gripped ridges and bumps. He lodged his bare toes into cracks in the rock. He knew he had to get to the top. He pushed with his legs and pulled with his hands. He was almost there. He reached up and grabbed the overhang of the cliff.

The wind screamed and blew against Jack, knocking him off balance. His feet slipped! He was dangling by one hand! "Jack!"

Jack opened his eyes. It was dark. He could

faintly see Annie in the moonlight. "Annie!" he whispered.

"We have to *go*," she said.

"Have to get *down*," said Jack. He closed his eyes. He was still hanging from the cliff.

Annie shook his shoulder. "Jack! Wake up!"

"Oh! Whoa . . ." Jack sat straight up. "Oh, man, I was hanging from a cliff in Egypt—you—"

"You were dreaming about our last mission," interrupted Annie. "Remember—you were hanging from a cliff, but everything turned out okay. We saved Koku. Remember? The little baboon?"

"Right . . . right," breathed Jack. He rubbed his eyes and looked at Annie. "What's going on? What time is it? Why are you awake?"

"We have to go to the woods," said Annie. "It's back."

"How do you know?" said Jack.

"I couldn't sleep," said Annie. "I was looking out my window and saw the streak of light—"

"That's it," said Jack, jumping out of bed. "Let's go. Are Mom and Dad awake?"

"No. If we leave now, we'll be back before they get up," said Annie. "Meet you outside." She slipped out of Jack's room.

Jack didn't even turn on his light. He changed into a pair of shorts and a T-shirt. He pulled on his socks and sneakers. He threw his notebook and pencil into his backpack. Then he tiptoed down the hall, down the stairs, and out the front door.

Annie was waiting on the porch. The sun was about to rise, and birds had started to chirp in the warm summer dawn.

"Ready," Jack whispered.

Jack and Annie left the front porch and stepped lightly over the wet grass of their front yard. They hurried up the sidewalk and crossed the street into the Frog Creek woods. As they walked between the dark trees, the purple-blue sky overhead was growing lighter. Birdsong filled the woods.

"I wonder where we'll go today," said Jack.

"And what will be the secret of greatness that makes the Ring of Truth glow?" Annie said. Then she began to speak in a dramatic voice, like a TV announcer. "What amazing person will Jack and Annie meet today?"

Jack laughed, then spoke dramatically, too. "And when will they sniff the mist-gathered-at-first-light-on-the-first-day-of-the-new-moon-on-the-Isle-of-Avalon?"

"And when they do, what great talent will they choose for themselves?" said Annie.

Jack laughed again and shook his head.

"Our lives are kind of crazy," said Annie.

"You think?" said Jack.

The chorus of birds grew louder as the pale gold of dawn filtered down through the trees. When Jack and Annie came to the tallest oak in the woods, they looked up into the branches.

The magic tree house was outlined against the sky. Without a word, Annie grabbed the rope ladder and started up. Jack followed.

Jack and Annie climbed into the shadowy tree house. A ray of sunlight slanted through a window. It shone directly on a sheet of paper lying on the wooden floor. On the paper, Jack had written the secrets of greatness they had learned on their last three missions:

HUMILITY

HARD WORK

MEANING AND PURPOSE

A gold ring, a tiny bottle, and a yellowed scroll lay next to the paper. Jack picked up the scroll, unrolled it, and read aloud:

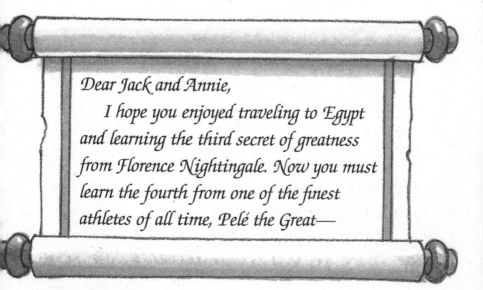

> Dear Jack and Annie,
>   I hope you enjoyed traveling to Egypt and learning the third secret of greatness from Florence Nightingale. Now you must learn the fourth from one of the finest athletes of all time, Pelé the Great—

"Pelé the Great?" said Jack. "He was a brilliant soccer player from Brazil."

"I know. Coach Cooney told us all about him," said Annie.

"This is so cool!" said Jack.

"Wait," said Annie. "There's more."

When you complete your mission, please come to Camelot before you return home.
—M.

"So, we're going to Camelot!" said Jack.

"Yep," said Annie. "And I wonder if we're going to Brazil, too." She and Jack looked around the tree house for a book that would help them on their journey.

"There!" said Annie. She picked up a pamphlet lying in a shadowy corner. "I don't believe it!"

"What? What?" said Jack.

"Look." Annie handed him the pamphlet.

"The World Cup!" said Jack. "That's the biggest sports event on the planet!"

"I know," said Annie. "Look, it's in Mexico! I've always wanted to go to Mexico." When she opened the pamphlet, she gasped. "And look what Merlin gave us." She held up two purple tickets.

"Mexico 70 Final?" said Jack, reading a ticket. "There are lots of games during the World Cup, but there's only one *final*."

"Thank you, Merlin!" said Annie with a laugh.

"So Pelé must be playing in the final!" Jack said.

"Yep." Annie shoved their tickets in her back pocket.

"Don't forget this," said Jack. He grabbed the small bottle lying on the floor and held it up to the sunlight. Sparkling mist swirled inside.

"Mist gathered at first light on the first day of the new moon on the Isle of Avalon," Jack said. Whenever he and Annie breathed in the mist and made a wish, they magically had a great talent for one hour. Jack tucked the bottle into his backpack.

Annie picked up the gold ring from the floor. "And here's the Ring of Truth," she said. "You get to wear it this time. Just make sure to keep your eye on it when we're with Pelé."

"Don't worry," said Jack as he slipped the ring onto his finger. The Ring of Truth would shine with a fiery light when they discovered the fourth secret of greatness.

"Let's go," said Annie.

"I still can't believe we're actually headed to

Soccer on Sunday

Mexico, to a *final* World Cup soccer game, to meet Pelé the Great," Jack said. "I mean, seriously?"

"Seriously," said Annie.

Jack pointed at the cover of their program. "I *seriously* wish we could go to Mexico City, 1970!"

The wind started to blow.

The tree house started to spin.

It spun faster and faster.

Then everything was still.

Absolutely still.

TWO

Lucky Ducks

The air in Mexico City was hot, humid, and smoggy. Jack heard screeching car tires, honking horns, and roaring truck motors. He looked at his clothes. He was wearing his own shorts and T-shirt. "Our clothes didn't change," he said.

"That's because kids wore shorts and T-shirts in the 1970s. Remember the photos of Mom and Dad?" said Annie.

"Right," said Jack. He and Annie looked out the window. The tree house had landed in a row of tall, leafy trees lining a busy street. Beyond the

branches was a jagged skyline with towers and tall buildings. Below the branches, traffic moved noisily up an avenue.

"It looks like we landed in the middle of

the city," said Jack. He opened their World Cup program to the first page and read:

> **Mexico City is one of the largest cities in the world. Its citizens are overjoyed that their city has been chosen to host the 1970 World Cup games. Held every four years, the games are played for several weeks. This year, sixteen countries will compete in the matches to determine the final winner.**

"And we've got tickets to see the final winner!" Jack said, grinning. "I wonder which two teams will be playing!" He thumbed through the booklet and saw page after page of black-and-white photos of the teams competing in the World Cup games. "Mexico, Belgium, Sweden, Israel, Italy, England . . ."

"Romania . . . West Germany . . . Brazil . . . ," Annie said, looking over his shoulder.

"There he is!" said Jack. "Arantes Nascimento—Pelé!"

"Well, we know Brazil made it to the final game,

or we wouldn't be here," said Annie. "But I wonder who they're playing."

"We'll soon find out." Jack closed the program. As he put it into his backpack, he saw his notebook and pencil, the bottle of magic mist—and some coins and bills inside. "Look, Mexican money—pesos. We have five- and ten-peso coins, and bills worth fifty pesos."

"Sounds like a lot," said Annie. "We can buy Mexican food when we get hungry. Tacos. Enchiladas. Burritos. I love Mexican food!"

"Who doesn't?" Jack said. "Who doesn't love *everything* we're about to do?" He pulled on his backpack and led the way down the rope ladder.

When Jack and Annie reached the ground, they saw a large white building with an American flag. Engraved on the front wall of the building were the words EMBASSY OF THE UNITED STATES. A uniformed guard stood under a green awning at the entrance.

"Perfect. We landed in front of the U.S. Embassy," said Jack.

"Why is that perfect?" asked Annie.

"A country's embassy is supposed to help its citizens when they visit another country," said Jack.

"Oh, that *is* perfect," said Annie. "Come on."

Jack and Annie headed toward the entrance. Before they got to the door, the guard stepped out from under the awning.

"Sorry, kids," he said. "The embassy is closed on Sundays." The man looked very formal in his blue uniform jacket and white hat and gloves, but he sounded friendly. He spoke with a Southern accent.

"Oh, we were just looking for information," said Jack. "We're Americans."

"Groovy. Where y'all from?" the guard asked.

"We're Jack and Annie from Frog Creek, Pennsylvania," said Annie.

"I'm Benny from Valdosta, Georgia," said the guard. "Pleased to meet you."

"Hi, Benny," said Jack. "We're going to the World Cup game that's being played today. And—"

"Lucky ducks!" Benny broke in. "It's going to be the game of a lifetime!"

"Game of a lifetime?" Jack said.

"Today's the final match—best two teams in the world. Italy's playing Brazil!" said Benny.

"Brazil? That's Pelé's team, right?" said Jack.

"Sure is," said Benny. "Pelé the Great."

Jack grinned at Annie. "This is *so* cool!" he said.

"No kidding!" said Annie.

"Y'all seem to really love soccer," said Benny.

"We do. We love to watch it and play it," said Annie.

"Well, y'all are unusual," said Benny. "Most American kids hardly know anything about soccer."

"Um . . . yeah . . . right," said Jack. His dad had told them that kids rarely played soccer when he was growing up.

"Don't worry," said Annie. "It'll become more popular with time. In fact, by 2014—"

"Excuse me," Jack interrupted, "but do you know when the match starts? And where it is?"

Benny looked at his watch. "Well, it's almost ten a.m. now," he said. "So you've got two hours till kickoff at Aztec Stadium. That's about ten miles south of here."

"Ten miles?" said Jack.

"Don't worry," said Benny. "Public transportation can get you there pretty fast. Just walk a few blocks to the Metro Insurgentes station. That's where you catch the metro."

"Metro?" said Jack.

"It's like what we'd call a subway train in the States," said Benny. "Y'all need to catch the Red Line in the direction of Pantitlán. And then—"

"Wait, please," said Jack. He pulled out his notebook and pencil. "Could you spell that?"

"Here, I'll write it down," said the guard.

Jack gave his notebook and pencil to Benny. The friendly guard mumbled the directions to himself as he wrote them down: "Walk to Metro Insurgentes . . . then Red Line to Pino Suaréz . . . then Blue Line to Taxqueña, last stop . . . then a tram to Aztec Stadium."

"It sounds complicated," said Jack.

"Just ask somebody if you get lost," said Benny.

"Folks here are super nice—they'll be glad to help." The guard handed the notebook and pencil back to Jack.

"Thanks," said Jack. He tore out the sheet with Benny's directions and put it in the pocket of his shorts.

"I hope y'all have seats for the game," said Benny. "From what I hear, it's completely sold out."

"Don't worry—we have tickets," said Annie. She showed them to Benny.

"Far out!" said Benny. "Y'all have two of the best seats in the house!"

"Really?" said Jack. He couldn't believe it.

"How in the world did you get these?" said Benny.

Annie shrugged. "We know somebody who knows somebody," she said.

"Well, don't let anybody see those tickets," said Benny. "People would sell their mothers for those seats."

Annie laughed as she put the tickets back in

her pocket. "So how do we get to the metro train, Benny?" she asked.

"Go up this street to the big statue of the angel, turn left onto Florencia, and after a couple of blocks, ask somebody to direct you to Insurgentes—that's *in-sur-HEN-tes*," said the guard, sounding out the word.

"Thanks, Benny! You've been a big help," said Annie.

"Yeah, thanks," said Jack.

"You're welcome! Anytime!" said the guard.

Jack put the program, notebook, and pencil back into his backpack. Then he and Annie waved good-bye and headed away from the embassy. When they got to the sidewalk, they looked up and down the busy avenue.

"There's the angel!" said Annie. She pointed to the huge statue of a winged angel looming in the distance.

"Good, it's not that far," said Jack.

The air was hot and humid and smelled like car exhaust. But Jack was so excited, nothing bothered him as he and Annie walked past banks, airline offices, and fancy hotels. When they reached the golden angel in the middle of a traffic circle, Jack checked Benny's directions, then looked around.

"There it is," he said, pointing to a sign that said FLORENCIA AVENUE. They hurried across the street and headed up Florencia.

"Benny said that when we get to this street, we should ask someone for help," said Annie. "Excuse me," she said to a woman waiting at a stoplight, "could you please tell us where we can find ..." She turned to Jack. "What was the name?"

"*In-sur-HEN-tes,*" Jack said, sounding it out like Benny had.

"Yes," said the woman with a smile. "Just past Londres Street." She pointed straight ahead.

"Thank you," said Annie. She and Jack started walking again.

"I can't believe this—we have the best seats in the stadium!" Jack said.

"It makes sense," said Annie. "Merlin gave us

those seats to help us with our mission."

"Right, like maybe Pelé will be playing near us and we'll get to meet him," said Jack. "Then somehow he'll reveal a secret of greatness. And then we go back to Camelot to meet up with Merlin!"

"We're *super*-lucky ducks," said Annie. "Quack-quack."

THREE

Hurry Up for the World Cup!

"Look, Insurgentes." Jack pointed to a sign on a large building that said MERCADO INSURGENTES. "That's it—the metro we're supposed to catch. Come on!"

Annie and Jack joined the crowd heading into the Insurgentes building. They strolled down a corridor between stalls selling ponchos, beaded bags, wooden animals, baskets woven with palm leaves, and silver jewelry—tons of silver jewelry. The smell of sizzling meat came from food stands. Nothing looked like a train or subway station.

Finally Jack stopped near a group of men in sombreros playing guitars, violins, and trumpets. He turned to Annie. "This doesn't feel right!" he yelled above the noise of the music.

"We must have made a mistake!" Annie yelled back.

"Let's get out of here," said Jack. "We're wasting time!" He and Annie turned and hurried back down the corridor between the stalls. They wove around shoppers until they escaped through the entrance of the giant market.

A soft, warm rain had started to fall.

"I don't get it," said Jack. He pointed to the sign on the building. "It says MERCADO INSURGENTES."

"Look at Benny's notes again," said Annie.

Jack pulled out their directions. "Oh, no!" he said. "Benny wrote *Metro* Insurgentes, not *Mercado* Insurgentes!"

"I'll ask for help!" said Annie. She took the directions and walked over to an old man reading a newspaper on a bench. "Excuse me, sir, where is Metro Insurgentes, please?"

Soccer on Sunday

The old man pointed up the street.

"Thanks!" said Annie. She ran back to Jack and handed him the sheet of directions. Jack stuffed it into his backpack.

"Hurry, or we'll be late!" Jack said.

Jack and Annie ran up the street through the warm, drizzling rain. They stopped when they came to an overpass jammed with trucks and cars. In a sunken plaza below was a round concrete building covered with posters and murals. One sign on the building said PLAZA INSURGENTES. Another said METRO STATION.

"That's it!" said Jack. He and Annie ran down to the plaza. They hurried by a fountain, vendors, and snack bars until they came to the rounded entrance of the metro.

When they stepped into the station, the noise was deafening, even louder than in the market. Hordes of people were rushing up and down the stairs. Jack and Annie joined the stream of traffic going down. Beyond the stairs was a row of turnstiles.

"How do we do this?" said Annie.

"Watch what everyone else is doing," said Jack.

One at a time, people were dropping a single coin into slots in the turnstiles and then passing through. Jack pulled two pesos out of his backpack and gave one to Annie. Copying everyone else, they passed through the turnstiles onto the metro platform.

"That wasn't so hard," said Annie.

Another huge crowd was waiting on the sweltering platform for the next train. Jack pulled out their directions again. "Red Line to Pino Suaréz!" he shouted to Annie above the noise. "Then the Blue Line to Taxqueña! Then we get off at the last stop and get a tram to Aztec Stadium!"

"Easy!" yelled Annie.

Really? thought Jack.

A train was rolling in. "Red Line?" Annie shouted to a woman.

As the woman nodded, the metro train came to a stop. The doors opened. As passengers spilled off the train, people on the platform surged forward.

Jack grabbed Annie's hand and they moved

with the crowd. But before they could even get close to the train, a bell rang and the doors slammed shut. The people left on the platform jumped back as the train pulled away.

"We'll get the next one!" Jack shouted.

Soon another train rolled in. Jack grabbed Annie's hand again, and they surged forward with the crowd. They were pushed and shoved as they tried to get through the doorway. Finally they were inside!

"Safe!" said Jack, collapsing onto a seat with Annie. But they were nearly squashed as more passengers piled into the metro. More and more kept cramming in, until people were practically sitting on Jack's and Annie's laps.

The bell rang. The doors closed. The train pulled away from the station. As it rumbled through the dark tunnel, the air in the car was suffocating. Jack could feel sweat trickling down his face and the back of his neck.

"What's our stop?" Annie yelled to Jack.

Jack reached into his back pocket. The paper

with the directions wasn't there. He wrestled his backpack off his back and looked inside. The sheet of paper wasn't there, either. "Do you have our directions?" he shouted at Annie.

"No! You had them!" said Annie.

"I must have dropped them!" said Jack, panicked.

"Don't worry," said Annie. "Excuse me!" she yelled up at a woman standing over them. "How do we get to the Aztec station?"

The woman shrugged. Then she asked a man, who asked another woman. But the train stopped and all three people hurried off without answering Annie's question!

"Should we get off, too?" asked Annie.

"I don't know!" said Jack. "We don't know if this is the right station! They're not announcing where we are!"

New passengers piled into the car, and the aisle became even more crowded. Once again, as the train took off, Jack and Annie were squashed in their seats by the crush of passengers in the aisle.

"Where is Aztec Stadium?" Jack yelled to no one in particular.

"Get off at Pino Suaréz!" a man shouted above the roar. The man said more, but Jack couldn't hear him. Before he could ask the man to repeat his directions, the train stopped—and the man pushed his way out the doors.

"Is this Pino Suaréz?" Jack shouted to Annie. He looked around wildly, trying to find a sign. "This is a nightmare!"

"Is this Pino Suaréz?" Annie yelled to a teenage girl with a large backpack.

"Sorry, I don't know," the girl said. "Check the

map!" She pointed to a large map on the far wall of the train.

"Let's look!" said Jack. But it was impossible to get to the map, as the aisle had already filled up with new passengers.

"Too late," said Annie.

The metro doors closed, and the train thundered on through the dark tunnel.

FOUR

Follow Me!

"Wait till we stop again!" Annie yelled at Jack.

"But what if we just missed our stop?" said Jack. "What if that was Pino Suaréz?"

"We're stopping again! We have to check that map!" said Annie.

As the train slowed for the next stop, Jack and Annie both got ready to jump out of their seats. But when the metro doors jerked open, hardly anyone got off. Instead, new travelers pushed their way into the crowded car. Jack and Annie hardly had room to breathe, much less stand up and check the map.

"No way!" Jack shouted to Annie.

"Can someone help us?" Annie called. "We need to get to the World Cup game! Where is the stop for Pino Suaréz?" Nobody seemed to hear her.

"This is hopeless!" said Jack.

Then he heard a small voice, shouting above the noise of the train. "Excuse me! Pardon me, please!"

A Mexican boy squeezed through the crowd to get to Jack and Annie. "Did you say you are going to the World Cup game?" he shouted.

"Yes!" said Annie.

"Me too!" said the boy. "Can I help you?"

"Yes!" said Jack, relieved. "We don't know where to get off!"

"The next stop! Pino Suaréz!" said the boy. "You can follow me!"

As soon as the train stopped, Jack and Annie followed the boy, squeezing past people to get to

the door. "Excuse me! Excuse me!" they said. Then all three of them popped off the hot, airless train. Half the people on the train got off with them.

"Man, that was crazy," said Jack. He was covered in sweat.

"Thank you!" Annie said to the boy.

"It's not over yet," the boy said, smiling. He had a cheerful, open face. "We have to catch the Blue Line to Taxqueña."

"Can we come with you?" asked Annie. "We lost our directions."

"Of course!" said the boy. "This way! *Pronto!*"

Jack and Annie followed the boy down a tunnel and around a corner to the Blue Line. Hordes of people were waiting for that metro line, too.

"My father told me to go to the end of the platform," said the boy. "The last train cars are never as crowded."

As the train rolled into the station, Jack and Annie quickly followed the boy down the platform. They sped up when the doors opened. Just before the doors closed again, the three of them jumped into the last car of the train.

The boy was right. The car wasn't crowded at all. They got good seats together. Jack felt hugely relieved.

"Thanks for helping us," he said.

"You're welcome," said the boy. "My name is Roberto." He held out his hand.

Jack shook Roberto's hand. "I'm Jack," he said.

"And I'm Annie," said Annie, shaking his hand, too. "Are you going to the game alone, Roberto?"

"Yes. My parents gave me a ticket for my birthday present," said Roberto. "It's the best present I've ever gotten."

"Is today your birthday?" asked Jack.

Roberto nodded. "I turn ten years old today."

"Happy birthday!" Jack and Annie said together.

"I'm ten, too," said Annie. "Jack's eleven."

"Why didn't your mom and dad come with you?" Jack said.

"They could only afford one ticket," said Roberto. "I have eight brothers and sisters. It will be my job to tell them everything I see. They will all be waiting at home for my stories about the great game." He smiled his big smile again.

The train began to slow down. "We get off here," said Roberto, standing up.

Jack and Annie followed Roberto off the metro, down an underground passageway, then out of the stifling station into the breezy, wet air. Jack felt a thousand times better.

Soccer on Sunday

"Now we take tramline 53," said Roberto.

"That's like a subway *above* ground, right?" said Jack.

"Yes. Come with me." Roberto led Jack and Annie across a walkway to the trolley tracks. Hundreds of people stood in lines, waiting to board the packed trams. As they joined one of the lines, Jack pulled out some pesos.

"Everyone's going to the World Cup champion-ship game," said Roberto. "People have come to Mexico from all over South America and Europe to see this game."

"Did you hear that it would be the game of a lifetime?" asked Jack.

"Absolutely," said Roberto.

"Did you know Pelé was playing?" Annie asked.

"Of course! Pelé the Great!" said Roberto. "He has made over a thousand goals. And his whole team is fantastic. They are called the Beautiful Team!"

"That's cool," said Jack.

"Three pesos," said the driver at the door of the tram.

Roberto reached into his pocket, but Jack stopped him. "I got it," he said. Jack handed over three pesos.

"Thank you, Jack," said Roberto. Then they all hopped aboard the tram bound for the World Cup championship game. There were no empty seats, so they stood in the aisle and held on to a pole. As the tram began to move, Jack, Annie, and Roberto huddled together and talked excitedly.

"Brazil has the best team in history," said Roberto. "But Italy has a great team, too. Did you hear the story of Italy playing West Germany in the semifinal match?"

"No. What happened?" said Annie.

"Even though Italy was behind, they never gave up," said Roberto. "Italy scored five goals in extra time!" He heaved a big sigh. "I can't believe it. I never thought in my life I would be here today to see this game."

"Me neither!" said Annie.

Jack laughed. "Not in a million years."

"We'll arrive at Aztec Stadium soon," said Roberto, looking out the window.

"Thanks for your help!" said Jack. He really liked this kid. He was also amazed that a ten-year-old could get around the city so easily. "Do you go to the stadium a lot?"

"No. This is my first time," he said. "But I have practiced this trip in my mind many times.

My father told me exactly what to do."

"Do you play soccer?" Annie asked.

"I try. But I am not that great," Roberto said.

"Me neither," said Annie. "I love it, but I'm not great."

"Same with me," said Jack. "Love it. Not great." And they all laughed.

By the time the tram arrived at the station near the stadium, the clouds had disappeared. Bright sunshine had replaced the drizzling rain. Steam was rising from a gigantic parking lot.

"That's Aztec Stadium," Roberto said, pointing out the window to an enormous concrete building.

"Cool," said Jack. He looked at his watch. "It's eleven-thirty-five."

"Twenty-five minutes until kickoff," said Roberto. "We made it!"

"All because of you, Roberto!" said Annie.

"Stay with me," the Mexican boy said with a smile, "and I'll take good care of you."

FIVE

High in the Sky

When the doors opened, Roberto led Jack and Annie off the tram. They walked down a ramp from the station and headed into the huge parking area.

"Aztec Stadium is named for the people who built an empire in this part of Mexico many hundreds of years ago," said Roberto.

"Really?" said Jack. He'd read about the Aztec Empire. He could imagine the enormous stadium being similar to an Aztec pyramid.

Thousands of spectators flooded the parking

lot. They wore bright summer clothes and wide-brimmed hats. Vendors walked among the big cars, selling Brazilian, Italian, and Mexican flags. Kids were waving souvenir programs, soccer shirts, and caps for sale.

Jack and Annie followed Roberto to the nearest entrance, and Annie held out their two tickets.

"That way, gate G!" a stadium official said. He pointed toward one of the other entrances.

When Roberto showed his ticket, the man pointed in the same direction.

"Hurray! I hope I'm sitting near you," said Roberto.

"Me too!" said Jack.

Jack, Annie, and Roberto followed a crowd through gate G and into the giant stadium. They all looked up at the stands. Dozens of tiers of seats rose above the green soccer field. The rows were so steep, it looked as if spectators in the highest rows might fall straight down onto the field.

"This place is huge!" said Jack.

"Where do we go now?" said Annie.

"My father said I should ask an official," said Roberto, looking around. "Over there!" He led Jack and Annie to an usher in uniform standing at the bottom of an aisle.

"Can you please tell us where our seats are?" Annie asked, showing her ticket to the woman.

When the woman looked at the ticket, her eyes grew wide. "You have some of the best seats in the stadium!" she said. She pointed to the section closest to the field. "Over there—second row, right on the aisle!"

"Yay!" said Jack. The guard at the embassy had been right. They *did* have incredible seats—seats that would help them get close enough to

Pelé to learn a secret of greatness from him.

Jack turned excitedly to Roberto. "Where's *your* seat?" he asked.

Roberto showed his ticket to the usher. "Where do I go?" he asked.

"Well ... you are in the same line as your friends ... ," the woman told Roberto.

"Fantastic!" he said with a big grin.

"But I'm afraid your seat is in a different section," said the usher. She pointed all the way up. "It's near the very top, high up in the sky."

The smile left Roberto's face, but then it returned. "I'd better go," he said. "It was great to meet you."

"You too," said Jack.

"Good-bye, Jack and Annie," said Roberto, and he started up the steep steps to the top of the stadium.

"Roberto, wait!" Annie called, and she hurried up the steps after him. Jack followed her. "Listen—I want to trade seats with you," she said. She held out her ticket.

Really? thought Jack. *What about our mission?*

"Oh, no! I cannot!" said Roberto.

"Yes, you can!" said Annie. "Please! We *have* to trade seats."

"But why?" asked Roberto.

"Because it's your birthday," said Annie. "And if you have a good seat, you can tell your eight brothers and sisters and your parents all about the game. So it will be like eleven people are getting a good seat. Not just one."

That actually makes sense, thought Jack. Still, he was amazed by Annie's generosity.

"But no, I cannot—" said Roberto.

"But yes, you *can,*" said Annie. She grabbed Roberto's ticket and put her own ticket in his hand. "You guys have fun!" She started up the stairs.

Jack felt a wave of guilt. "Wait, stop. That's not fair," he said to Annie. "Maybe I should give up *my* seat."

"No, it's okay. I'll give up mine," said Annie.

Roberto laughed. "You are both too kind," he

said. "I cannot take either of your seats." Roberto handed Annie her ticket and took his back.

"No, please, I want—" Annie protested.

"Wait, I have another idea," Jack said to Annie. "We can take turns. I'll switch with Roberto for the first half. And you switch with him for the second half."

"Perfect!" said Annie. "That way, Roberto can get a great view of the whole game. And you and I will each get a great view for half the time."

"Right." Jack pulled the Ring of Truth off his finger. He slipped it into Annie's hand and spoke softly to her. "The person who's sitting close to the field should wear this. Be sure to check it if you think you've discovered Pelé's secret."

"Got it," Annie said, putting the ring on her finger. "I'll give it back to you at halftime."

"Right," said Jack. "How long is halftime, Roberto?"

"Fifteen minutes."

"Plenty of time," said Jack. He looked at his seat number. "A-26. Okay, I'll find you at seat

A-26, Annie. Wait for me." Then he swapped tickets with Roberto.

"Thank you a million times, Jack!" said Roberto.

"No problem," said Jack. "See you guys later!" And he started up the stairs.

"Have fun in the sky!" called Annie.

"I will!" Jack felt great as he started up the steps to the top of the stands. He was sure he'd done the right thing, especially since it was Roberto's birthday.

But as Jack climbed higher and higher, his spirits fell. The stands were so high, he wondered if he'd be able to see *anything*. By the time he reached the top rows, he was out of breath. He showed his ticket to an usher, and she pointed toward his seat.

Jack squeezed past people and collapsed on the bench. From his seat, the field looked a million miles away. *How can anyone enjoy the game from up here?* he wondered. He wished huge stadium screens had been invented so *everyone* could see the game well.

Soccer on Sunday

The spectators around Jack seemed to be having a good time anyway. A couple and their two children were eating tacos and drinking sodas. Others were waving small multicolored flags. A teenage boy next to Jack was looking through a pair of large binoculars. A man with a bushy mustache held a scratchy-sounding portable radio.

Jack could hear the sportscaster through the static: *"Final World Cup championship! A billion people around the world are watching on television! And over a hundred thousand spectators are here in Aztec Stadium today!"*

"Here they come!" shouted the boy looking through binoculars.

Suddenly all the spectators let out a roar. The two soccer teams were running onto the field.

"Italy's incredible team has blue shirts and white shorts!" the teenager with binoculars shouted. "Brazil's Beautiful Team: yellow shirts, blue shorts! Pelé is number ten!"

Jack couldn't see the colors of any uniforms, much less any numbers.

"Kickoff! And there Pelé goes!" the commentator on the crackly radio yelled. *"Pelé! There! There!"*

Where? Where? Jack wondered. He really wanted to see Pelé the Great, but from his seat high up in the sky, the players on the field looked no bigger than ants.

The radio commentator shouted excitedly about the game. Jack could only catch pieces of what he was saying: *"What a pass! . . . Carlos Alberto, captain of Brazil's team! . . . Hitting a very long ball! . . . Dangerous free-kick situation! . . . Italy, zero, Brazil, zero!"*

With every play, everyone in the huge stadium screamed, whistled, cheered, or booed. Then thousands of Brazil fans jumped to their feet, pumping their fists in the air and screaming, "Gooooaaaallll!!!!" Jack jumped to his feet, too. The teenager with the binoculars shouted, "Pelé leaped past the defender! He hit the ball and scored!"

Jack shook his head. He couldn't believe he'd

missed seeing Pelé make a goal! He really wished he had binoculars. He really, *really* wished he were sitting with Annie and Roberto!

Everyone sat down. Jack listened as carefully as he could to the voice of the radio commentator: *"Free kick! ... Way, way up! ... Beautiful! No wonder Brazil is called the Beautiful Team! ... Punching that one away! ... Dead ball!"*

Nothing the sportscaster said sounded like a secret of greatness to Jack. He just hoped Annie was paying close attention to the game and checking the ring a lot.

Even though he was envious, Jack was still glad that Roberto had a great view of the game. *If he was sitting up here*, Jack thought, *he'd have nothing to report to his eight brothers and sisters.*

Suddenly thousands of Italy fans leapt to their feet, screaming, and the older kid with binoculars shouted, "Italy scores! Brazil, one! Italy, one!"

Jack couldn't wait to switch seats with Annie

and watch the game up close! If the ring hadn't glowed for her, it would all be up to him. As soon as the radio announcer said, "Halftime!" Jack looked at his watch. It was 12:45. He had fifteen minutes to find Annie and Roberto. Jack squeezed past the people sitting in his row and took off down the mountain of stairs.

SIX

Annie? Roberto?

Jack raced down the steep stadium steps, trying to get ahead of the crowd. But by the time he reached the middle section, he had to slow down. The aisle was packed with people buying sodas and flags and soccer caps from vendors.

Jack couldn't get past the human traffic jam. He kept looking at his watch as he waited for the steps to clear. After almost five minutes, he squeezed through a gap in the crowd. *"A-26, A-26!"* he repeated as he struggled to get down to the sections near the playing field.

Finally Jack reached the last rows of section A. "Annie? Roberto?" he whispered. As he looked down the steep rows of seats, all the wide-brimmed hats made it impossible to see.

"Annie! Roberto!" Jack yelled. "Annie! Roberto!"

There was no sign of them anywhere. Jack hadn't expected all the hats—or all the people milling around, standing, stretching, talking to neighbors, coming and going.

Jack looked at his watch again. There were five minutes left until the end of halftime. Stadium officials were telling everyone to return to their seats. "Take your seats! Halftime's almost over! Take your seats!"

Jack didn't know what to do. Suddenly he was caught in another traffic snarl as people started climbing back up to the higher tiers. "Keep moving!" an usher shouted at everyone. "Keep moving!"

A huge roar came from the crowd. The players were taking their positions again!

Kickoff! The second half of the game began! The Brazilian and Italian soccer stars were running in all directions. Even peering through the crowd, Jack loved watching them up close!

Suddenly an usher was by his side. "Where's your ticket?" the man asked.

Now's my chance! thought Jack. He showed his ticket. "Please help me. I'm looking for A-26," he said. "My sister—"

"A-26? That's not your seat! Your seat's at the top!" the stadium official said. "Please go there now!"

"But—" started Jack.

"There's no time!" barked the frazzled man. "The game has started again! Go back to your seat!"

Jack did as the official said. *Annie won't know why I didn't show up,* he thought as he climbed the steep steps. *She'll be really worried.* He kept peering back down at the first rows of section A, looking for Annie and Roberto.

Finally Jack arrived back at the top of the stadium. He felt frustrated and anxious as he sat down in his seat. Not only would he *never* get a good look at the World Cup players now—but how was he going to find Annie again? Jack wished he had a cell phone, but he knew cell phones hadn't been invented yet. *How did people ever find each other in 1970?* he wondered.

As the fans of the Brazilian team kept whistling and cheering, Jack caught more snatches of the radio commentary: *"Brazil attacks! . . . Gerson scores long, low shot! . . . Brazil keeps attacking, passing, dribbling. . . ."*

Jack barely listened to the game anymore. He was too worried about what to do when it was over. *If the stadium was hectic at halftime, it'll be insane when the championship game ends,* he thought. He had Merlin's magic mist in his backpack. Should he use it now? he wondered. What great talent would help him find Annie? What great talent would help them accomplish their mission?

"Pelé follows with a hard shot!" the radio commentator's voice crackled. *"Here comes Alberto!"*

As the game went on, Jack couldn't stop worrying about finding Annie. *She must be wor-*

ried about finding me, too, he thought. *Knowing her, she might have tried to get help from the ushers or stadium guards. Maybe she talked to the police.* Jack looked up and down the aisles for any officials who might be searching for him.

"*Four minutes left!*" the announcer finally yelled.

"Tostao gets the ball!" the teenager with binoculars yelled. "Someone passes to Pelé! . . . Now Jairzinho has it! Brazil drives the ball and scores!"

As soon as it's over, I'll find seat A-26, Jack thought. *I'll keep looking as long as I have to!* Jack just hoped Annie would wait at her seat. He hoped she had discovered the secret of greatness during the game. He hoped Roberto would stick around and take them back to the U.S. Embassy.

Jack's thoughts were interrupted by a huge roar from the crowd.

"*Final score four to one! . . . The Beautiful Team has won! . . . Champions of the world! . . . Best World Cup of all time!*"

All the spectators around Jack were screaming and jumping up and down and hugging each other.

As Jack squeezed past the people in his row, the sportscaster shouted from the radio, *"Spectators are pushing past police and news reporters! Mobs are rushing onto the field. They're tearing off the players' shirts, their shoes! The fans have gone wild!"*

Soccer on Sunday

Jack hoped that Annie wouldn't get impatient in all the chaos and leave her seat to look for him. They'd *never* find each other if they were *both* moving around!

"Pelé's team members have hoisted him onto their shoulders! Celebrations will go on for days! The players will be honored at a giant banquet tonight in Mexico City!"

"Excuse me, excuse me," Jack mumbled as he tried to move past people in his row. He made his way through the crowd of celebrating fans and started down the steep stairs. He was bumped and pushed by people spilling from the stands. He moved as quickly as he could so he wouldn't get trampled.

Finally Jack reached the lower section of seats. As he looked around, he was accidentally knocked over by rowdy teenagers dancing in the aisle, screaming and waving flags. He scrambled back to his feet and jumped onto a stadium bench.

Finally Jack saw them: Annie and Roberto. They were only a few rows in front of him. They, too, were standing on a bench. But they were facing the field, pumping their arms in the air and shouting and cheering along with the crowd.

Jack was flooded with relief—but then he felt

angry. *What the heck?* he thought. Annie wasn't searching for him at all! She didn't seem to be a bit worried. She looked like she was having a great time!

"Annie!" Jack yelled. He hurried down to her. "Annie!"

When Annie and Roberto turned and saw Jack, they waved happily. "Oh, Jack, I'm so glad to see you!" Annie shouted. "We waited for you! But when you didn't come back, we figured your seat must have been okay! I hope it was!"

"Well, actually—" Jack shouted.

"Thanks *so* much for letting me keep my seat for the whole game!" Annie shouted. "Roberto and I had the best time! The game was incredible!"

"Yes, Jack!" shouted Roberto. "I had the best time of my whole life! But I was worried about you—I hope your seat in the sky was good!"

Jack took a deep breath. And then, for the second time that day, he chose to do the right thing: "Yeah, sure. My seat was good," he said with a sigh. "It was fine, totally fine."

SEVEN

Bye, Pelé

"I'm so glad!" shouted Annie. "Come and squeeze in here with us to watch! Everyone has gone crazy!"

Jack climbed up onto the bench and stood between Annie and Roberto as they watched the happy celebration on the field. The president of Mexico presented a giant trophy to Brazil, and Carlos Alberto, the captain of the team, lifted it high above his head.

"Yay, Brazil!" shouted Roberto. "Yay, Pelé!"

"Did the Ring of Truth ever glow?" Jack asked Annie. "When you were watching Pelé up close,

did you learn a secret of greatness from him?"

"No, not yet," Annie said. "Yay, Pelé!"

"Not *yet*?" said Jack. "Then when?"

"Don't worry," said Annie. "We still have time." She pulled the ring off her finger. "Here, you can wear it again."

Jack slipped the ring back onto his finger. *But what's the use?* he thought. *We lost our big chance. How can we ever get close to Pelé now?*

Followed by hundreds of photographers and TV cameras, the Beautiful Team was marching around the field. Confetti and streamers floated down from the stands. Firecrackers were whistling and popping over the stadium. Flag bearers waved huge green, yellow, and blue Brazilian flags. A band was playing.

Annie and Roberto clapped in rhythm to the music. Trying to hide both his worry and his disappointment, Jack clapped with them.

"They're leaving now!" said Roberto.

Police were leading Pelé and all the other Brazilian players off the crazy, crowded field.

TV cameras, reporters, and a mob of fans followed the World Cup champions.

"We should follow the team, too," Annie said to Jack. "Want to?"

"We *have* to," Jack said sharply. "We still have a mission to accomplish, remember?"

"Come with us, Roberto!" said Annie. "Let's all follow the team! *Pronto!*"

They climbed down from the bench and started running across the huge green soccer field. The parade of fans and players was leaving by the farthest exit.

"We'll catch up to them outside the stadium," said Roberto, running alongside Jack and Annie. "If I could get even twenty feet from Pelé, I would be happy forever!"

"Me too!" said Annie. "Jack and I have a question for him!"

No kidding, thought Jack.

Jack, Annie, and Roberto hurried through the exit, leaving Aztec Stadium and heading into the parking lot.

"Over there! They're getting on a bus!" said Roberto.

Not far away, fans and media were swarming around a bus. Photographers were snapping pictures, one after another, flashbulbs blazing. TV reporters were shouting questions at the team. Supporters were cheering and waving flags.

"Hurry!" cried Jack.

They all ran faster, but before they could get to the bus, it pulled away from the crowd. Police pushed fans out of its path so it could leave.

"Good-bye!" said Annie.

"Good-bye, Pelé!" Roberto yelled.

Jack, Annie, and Roberto watched the bus move out of the giant parking lot of Aztec Stadium.

Well, there goes our chance to accomplish our mission, Jack thought dismally. *There will be no reason to journey to Camelot now. It'll be the first time we've ever failed.*

"Don't worry," Annie said to him, as if she'd read his mind. "I'll bet the team's headed to the city. Let's go back there and look for them."

"Okay. I guess that might work," said Jack, trying not to give up hope. "I heard on the radio they were all going to a banquet in Mexico City tonight."

"Cool!" said Annie. "Someone's bound to know where that banquet is. Then maybe we can use our magic mist to get into the party."

"What? Like, make a wish to be the greatest party crashers in the world?" said Jack.

Annie laughed. "Whatever it takes," she said. She turned to Roberto and asked, "Roberto, can you help us get back into the city?"

"Of course! I owe you everything!" he said.

"Not really," said Jack. "Everyone deserves a good birthday."

"Thank you, Jack!" said Roberto with a big grin. "Come with me!"

Jack and Annie followed Roberto away from the giant concrete building, through the crowded parking lot, and toward the tramline.

"Whoa!" said Annie.

Thousands of people were waiting to board the

trams. "We will have to wait many hours to get one," said Roberto.

"Is there another station nearby?" Jack asked.

"Yes, but it will be just as crowded," Roberto answered.

"What do you think we should do?" Annie asked.

"I have an idea," said Roberto. "My great-aunt lives in a neighborhood north of here. Near her house, there is a bus stop. Want to give it a try?"

"Sure," said Jack. "We don't have another choice." He and Annie followed Roberto away from the tram station.

Clouds had moved back in. A soft rain fell as they walked along a road crowded with cars leaving the stadium. Horns were blaring and drivers were shouting at each other.

"This way," said Roberto, and he led Jack and Annie away from the busy road into a run-down neighborhood. They passed St. Anthony's Church, a junk store, a Laundromat, and a beauty shop.

Then Roberto led them down a dirt path between rows of stucco houses.

In the light rain, families sat on front porches. Several were listening to portable radios. The announcer was repeating the news about the World Cup final.

At the end of the street was a vacant lot filled with kids. When Jack, Annie, and Roberto drew closer, they saw about twenty boys and girls of all ages running around barefoot and covered with

mud. The kids were playing soccer. The goal lines had been marked off with tattered nets.

A grown-up on the sideline was acting as a referee. He blew a whistle and yelled, *"Halftime!"* All the kids stopped running. Several players walked away from the field as the others gathered in small groups to talk.

"Hey, Roberto!" An older boy waved.

"Hey, Miguel!" Roberto waved back.

"What are you doing here?" shouted Miguel.

"I'm taking my friends back to the city," Roberto answered. "We're going to catch the bus."

"Hey, Roberto!" another kid yelled.

"Hey, Diego!"

"Did you hear Brazil just won?" called Diego.

"Yay!" Roberto pumped the air with his fist. "Pelé the Great!" Then he turned to Jack and Annie. "I played ball with these kids once when I was visiting my aunt. If they come over, please do not tell them we just saw the World Cup final. It would make them sad that they could not afford to go."

"Okay, we won't," said Annie.

Jack nodded. Again he was impressed by Roberto's kindness. The boy seemed to care about everyone's feelings.

"Roberto, can your friends play soccer?" Miguel yelled. "Our team just lost some players for the second half!"

Before Roberto could answer, another boy jumped in. "No, Miguel! Not Roberto! Remember that time he played? He was the worst player ever!"

"Yeah, Miguel, remember?" yelled a tall girl. "He made us lose big-time!"

"I didn't ask *Roberto* to play, Carla!" Miguel said. "I asked if his two *friends* could play! We lost our three forwards, but we can play with two."

Jack glanced at Roberto. The boy's smile was gone and he stared at the ground.

"No way," Annie said to Jack, gritting her teeth. "Not in a million years."

"Right. Not even if we didn't have a mission and were the best players in the world," said Jack. "Come on, Roberto. Let's get out of here."

"Wait . . . wait a minute," said Annie. Then she turned back to the kids and yelled, "Yes, Miguel! We can play!"

"Are you crazy?" Jack asked her.

"We'll play on your team!" Annie yelled again to Miguel. "But only if you'll let Roberto play, too! All three of us want to be forwards!"

Roberto shook his head. "No, not me. They don't want me."

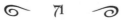

"I'm not that great, either," said Jack. "Annie, what's wrong with you?"

"What's wrong with me? Nothing!" Annie reached into Jack's backpack and took out the small bottle of Merlin's magic mist. "In fact, everything's about to be great—for all three of us!"

EIGHT

Game of a Lifetime

"Seriously?" said Jack.

"Yes!" said Annie.

"But what about our mission? Getting into the banquet? Meeting the players?" said Jack.

"Right now, *this* seems more important, don't you think?" said Annie.

Jack looked at Roberto's sad face. He thought about the boy's kindness and his happy excitement at the stadium. "Yeah," he said. "Yeah, it does." He turned and yelled at Miguel, "We'll play! But *all* of us! Or *none* of us!"

"Oh . . . okay," Miguel said reluctantly.

Roberto shook his head. "No, Jack, no," he said.

Diego's players laughed. "You'll lose now for sure, Miguel!" one of them yelled. "Big-time!"

"Give us a minute!" Jack said to the soccer players. And he huddled with Annie and Roberto.

"Jack, they are right. I'm not a good player," said Roberto.

"Me neither," said Jack. "But together we will make a beautiful team. I promise."

"Listen, Roberto," said Annie. "We'll use magic from Merlin the magician of Camelot and make a wish—"

"To play like Pelé," finished Jack.

"Magic?" said Roberto.

"Yes. Mist gathered at first light on the first day of the new moon on the Isle of Avalon," Annie said.

Roberto shrugged. "Okay," he said.

"Are you guys playing or not?" Miguel shouted.

"We're playing!" Jack yelled over his shoulder. He pulled the cork from the bottle and breathed in Merlin's magic mist. He smelled oranges and cinnamon and cedar. "I wish to play like Pelé!" he whispered.

Jack gave the tiny bottle to Annie. She breathed in the mist and said, "I wish to play like Pelé!"

Annie gave the bottle to Roberto, and he breathed in the magic mist. Then he exclaimed with great enthusiasm, "I wish to play like Pelé!"

"Come on!" Miguel shouted from the soccer field.

"We're coming! One second!" said Jack. He put Merlin's magic mist away and glanced at his watch. "It's three-fifteen now. We have one hour of magic. At four-fifteen the magic ends. Let's go!"

Jack confidently led Annie and Roberto toward the soccer game. When they got to the edge of the field, Jack stopped. "Off with the shoes," he said cheerfully. The three of them slipped off their shoes and socks to be like the other kids.

Jack left his backpack next to his shoes. Then he clapped his hands. "Okay!" he said. "Let's play ball!"

As Jack, Annie, and Roberto walked onto the

field, mud oozed between their toes. The rain had stopped, but the ground was soaked. They took forward positions on Miguel's team.

"We're ahead by two goals," said Miguel. "Don't blow it, okay?"

Jack just smiled and nodded. Buzzing with excitement, he was eager to play. The referee placed the soccer ball in the center of the muddy field. A kicker and another teammate from Diego's team stood near the ball.

On the other side of the centerline, the opposite team glared at the three forwards. But Jack wasn't worried. He grinned back at them, eager for the game to start.

The referee on the dusty sideline blew a whistle, and the second half of the match began.

The kicker on Diego's team tapped the ball to her teammate, who passed it to Diego. As Diego and some other teammates knocked the ball around, Jack noticed that they were really good soccer players. But then suddenly Annie slipped in and stole the ball from them.

She whacked it with her instep, passing it to Jack, who slid it to Roberto.

Roberto began moving the ball down the field. As Diego's defenders moved in, Roberto changed pace from slow to fast, slow to fast. The ball seemed glued to his feet, until he fired a shot and drove it like a missile into the net.

"Score!" shouted the referee.

"Gooooaaaallll!!!!" Jack, Annie, and Roberto shouted, pumping the air with their fists.

All the other players gasped in amazement. "Who *are* you guys?" Carla shouted.

The goalie kicked the ball back into play. Carla passed it to a girl, who tried to pass it to a boy. But like lightning, Jack moved in and shot the ball through the air to Roberto.

Roberto used his thigh to pop the ball to Annie.

Annie stopped the ball with her foot and dribbled it past two defenders down the field, then passed it to Jack.

Jack moved the ball backward, forward, and sideways with short taps of his feet. He had never had so much fun in his life! He felt as if his feet could do anything! He saw Roberto across the field and kicked the ball to him, passing it over the heads of the defenders.

Roberto gave the ball a leaping header, sending it to Annie. Annie trapped the ball on the ground, then ran with it, keeping it close. She faked a move one way, then another, then kicked the ball backward to Roberto. Roberto delivered another perfect shot into the net.

"Score!"

"Gooooaaaallll!!!!" Jack, Annie, and Roberto shouted, pumping the air with their fists.

The goalie kicked the ball back into play. The opposing side started the ball down the muddy field, but Jack moved faster—he intercepted it and passed it to Annie. Annie sent the ball back to Roberto, who scooped his foot under the ball and popped it over a group of players, right to Jack. Jack outjumped two defenders and hit the ball with his chest, sending it down the field. Roberto sped after the ball, stole it from two players, and

gave it a swift kick—right into the net.

"Gooooaaaallll!!!!" Jack, Annie, and Roberto shouted, pumping the air with their fists.

"Gooooaaaallll!!!!" echoed the kids on Miguel's team *and* Diego's team! *All* the players seemed to be enjoying the work of the Beautiful Team of Jack, Annie, and Roberto.

As the game went on, everyone was playing really well. But Diego's players were no match for Jack, Annie, and Roberto. The three of them were like a goal-scoring machine.

Hearing the shouting and cheering from the soccer game, people left their porches and yards and hurried over to see the match.

The spectators watched Jack, Annie, and Roberto move like dancers, making low free kicks, long-range kicks, and leaping headers. They watched them hit the ball with their right and left feet, their foreheads, and their chests, stomachs, and thighs. They watched them dribble the ball down the field by tapping it with both feet, and send knuckleballs zigzagging across the dirt into the net.

In the final seconds of the game, everyone watched Jack execute a perfect bicycle kick. Like an acrobat, he threw his legs up in the air and kicked an overhead ball to Annie, who sent it on to Roberto, who shot it past the goalie into the net!

"Score!"

All the spectators, all the players, and even the referee pumped their fists in the air and screamed, "Gooooaaaallll!"

Then the referee blew the final whistle. "Game over!" he shouted.

There was a huge roar from the spectators.

"What's the score?" someone shouted from the crowd.

"Who cares?" said the referee. "That was *amazing!*"

All the players from both teams had big smiles on their wet, dirty faces. They were slapping each other on the back. Miguel and Diego picked up Roberto and carried him on their shoulders.

Other players gathered around Jack and Annie, asking for their autographs. A teenager took pictures of them with her instant camera. An old man shook their hands, saying, "You three are the Beautiful Team!" In the middle of the noisy celebration, Annie shouted to Jack, "What time is it?"

"Five minutes to four," he said, glancing at his watch.

"We'd better go. Remember Coney Island and Thebes," said Annie.

Soccer on Sunday

"Oh, yeah. Definitely," said Jack. On their last two missions, they'd found themselves in big trouble when their magic hour of greatness had ended.

Jack and Annie turned to Roberto, who was now holding a toddler, posing for the camera. After the picture was taken, Jack leaned close and said, "We have to leave fast before the magic wears off and we turn into our regular selves."

"Okay," said Roberto. He gave the child back to her mother. "Let's go to the city. But I warn you—they will all follow us!"

"Then let's go while we're still great athletes—and runners!" said Annie.

The three of them turned back to the crowd and waved. "Bye!" Jack, Annie, and Roberto said, backing up.

Everyone shouted at once, "No, wait!" "Don't go!" "Stay!" "Stay!"

"Sorry, but we have to go!" said Annie. "Thank you so much for letting us play!"

Jack grabbed his backpack. All three grabbed their shoes and socks. "Run!" yelled Roberto. And they took off running away from the soccer field.

Kids from both teams ran after them. The kids were all shouting, "Stop!" "Come back!" "Join our team!" "Join *our* team!"

But the Beautiful Team kept running. Using their magic skills, they jumped barefoot over a crumbling stone wall and leapfrogged over a row of garbage cans.

"Wait!" "Don't leave us!" The soccer kids kept chasing after them.

"This way!" Roberto led Jack and Annie down an alley and out to a dirt road. The three of them ran between rows of cinder-block buildings. They zipped around a maze of sheets and towels hanging on clotheslines. They jumped over potholes and smelly garbage. As they kept running and leaping, Jack felt as if he were flying. He felt agile and light-footed.

Then suddenly Jack felt heavy and clumsy. Out of breath, he slowed down and came to a stop. Annie and Roberto did the same. Covered with mud, the three of them collapsed onto the ground.

Soccer on Sunday

"I—I—can't run anymore . . . ," Jack said.

"Me neither," said Annie.

"I'm dead," said Roberto.

Jack looked at his watch. "Seventeen minutes after four," he said breathlessly. "Our magic hour is over."

NINE

GOOOOAAAALLLL!!!!

"So now—we—we can just be our old selves again," said Roberto, panting.

There were no signs of the soccer kids. As Jack looked around, he saw a newspaper stand and an outdoor café. "Hey, are you guys as hungry and thirsty as I am?" he asked.

"Yes!" Annie and Roberto said together.

Jack pulled some pesos out of his backpack. "How are we doing here?" he said. He showed his money to Roberto. "Do we have enough for tacos and bus fare, too?"

Roberto nodded, grinning.

"Perfect," said Jack. "Let's grab a bite. Then Annie and I have to find a big banquet in the city."

"Really? Do you not need to wash up first?" asked Roberto.

"Oh, yeah . . ." Jack sighed as he looked at his mud-splattered clothes.

"Let's worry about that after we eat," said Annie.

The three of them stood up and headed inside the café. A heavyset woman with brown skin and gray hair was frying food behind a counter. A couple of teenagers were putting coins in a jukebox. Loud music started to play.

"Three taco plates and three lemonades, please," Roberto said to the woman behind the counter.

She nodded and put food onto three plates. Then she brought the plates to a table and set them down. Soon she delivered three tall glasses of pink lemonade.

Jack, Annie, and Roberto dug hungrily into their food. Jack gobbled up tacos filled with tomatoes, chilies, and cheese. He ate a big serving of black beans and yellow rice and gulped down his lemonade.

"Roberto, you scored lots of goals today," Annie said, her mouth full.

"Yeah, your feet moved like lightning," said Jack.

Roberto laughed. "You two made me look good," he said. "You passed the ball to me every chance you got."

"That's called teamwork," said Annie.

"Yes, it is!" said Jack. "Someone called us the Beautiful Team!"

"Right!" said Annie. She raised her arms above her head. "Yay, Beautiful Team!" she exclaimed.

Roberto laughed. "You have a good enthusiasm for soccer, Jack and Annie," he said. "Enthusiasm is everything."

Jack smiled. "Right, and now I have enthusiasm for eating this food," he said.

"Me too! It's so good!" said Annie, taking another bite of rice and beans.

"Hey, Jack, where did you get that ring?" asked Roberto. "It looks like it's on fire."

"*What?*" said Jack and Annie together. They both looked at the ring on Jack's finger. It was flickering with light.

"Oh, man," whispered Jack.

Annie's eyes grew huge. "What were we just talking about?" she asked.

"Uh—good food," said Jack.

"Jack's bicycle kick," said Roberto.

"The Beautiful Team," said Annie.

"Enthusiasm," said Roberto. "I said, 'Enthusiasm is everything.'"

Suddenly the ring exploded with light.

"That's it!" cried Jack.

"*Enthusiasm is everything!*" said Annie. "Roberto, I think you just said something amazing and true and—"

"And *great!*" said Jack.

"But it wasn't me who first said it," said Roberto. "Pelé said it."

"*Pelé* said that?" said Jack.

"Yes. My father read it in the newspaper," said Roberto. "Pelé said when you play soccer, 'enthusiasm is everything.'"

"Okay, that's it, we just accomplished our mission!" said Annie.

"We can go to Camelot now!" said Jack. They both shot their arms in the air and shouted, "GOOOOAAAALLLL!!!!"

"What mission? Where's Camelot?" asked Roberto. He looked confused.

"It's a long story," said Jack.

"Just know that you helped us discover a really important secret of greatness from Pelé," said Annie. *"Thank you!"*

Roberto smiled. "You're welcome!" he said. But then the smile left his face. "I am happy. But I am sad, too," he said.

"Why are you sad?" asked Annie.

"Today was a magical day," said Roberto. "But it will never happen again. I will never be a great soccer player again."

"Yes, you *can* be a great soccer player again," Annie said. "You have lots of enthusiasm."

"That's all I have," said Roberto. "I'm clumsy. I don't run fast or kick well. Before today, I never scored even one goal."

"Roberto. This is really important," said Annie. "If you want to be a great soccer player—"

"Or great at *anything*," Jack broke in.

"Right. If you want to be great at anything, there

are four secrets you need to know," said Annie.

"Right," said Jack. "First, you need to have *humility*—that means you have to be willing to learn from others."

"Roberto has that," said Annie.

"Absolutely you have that," Jack said to Roberto. "Second, being great takes *hard work*."

"Do you work hard at practicing soccer?" Annie asked Roberto.

"Well, no . . . ," said Roberto.

"I don't, either," said Jack. "Okay, so we should both start practicing more."

"Third, you need to have *meaning and purpose* in your life," said Annie.

Roberto frowned. "What does that mean?" he said.

"That means you try to do something that's good for the world, and not just yourself," said Annie.

"Oh!" said Roberto. "Well, soccer does that. It brings people together from different neighborhoods. And today it brought people together from all over the world in the stadium!"

"And it brought the three of us together," said Annie.

"Good," said Jack. "And finally, *enthusiasm.* And enthusiasm is something we know you have."

"Yes!" said Roberto. Smiling again, he settled back in his seat. "So I know the thing I must do. I must start to practice very hard. My brothers and sisters will help me with that. . . . Oh. Oh, no!" He jumped up from his chair.

"What's wrong?" said Annie.

"I must go now!" Roberto said. "I forgot all about my family. Everyone will be waiting to hear my stories about the game!"

"Oh, right! We have to go, too," said Jack, standing up with Annie. Jack looked at their bill and left a bunch of pesos on the table. Then they all headed out of the café.

The rain had let up and there was a steamy mist in the air.

"Where is the banquet you must find?" said Roberto.

"Oh, we don't have to go there anymore," said

Jack. "Our mission is done. We just need to get back to the U.S. Embassy."

"No problem," said Roberto. "The bus goes to the Insurgentes station, very near the embassy. We can all get off there, and I'll catch the metro to my neighborhood. Come on!" He led Jack and Annie across a vacant lot. Then they started up a dirt road lined with small stucco houses.

"There it is! Run!" Roberto said.

An old bus was rattling up the road. Jack and Annie ran with Roberto to the corner. Out of breath, they got to the bus stop just in time. The doors of the bus opened, and the three of them hopped aboard.

"Metro Insurgentes, please," Jack said to the driver. He paid for three fares. Then, even though there were plenty of seats, Jack, Annie, and Roberto squeezed into a two-seater so they could all sit together.

As the bus wound through the outskirts of Mexico City, Jack leaned his head against the window. Soon he closed his eyes. . . . The next thing he knew, he was back in the game—kicking the ball forward, backward, and sideways . . . jumping into the air . . . lobbing the ball past defenders, past the goalie, and into the net! Jack held a trophy high above his head while the crowd roared. . . .

"Wake up, kids! We're here!" announced the bus driver.

Jack opened his eyes. The bus driver was standing over them. They'd all fallen asleep on the long ride back to the city.

Annie gently shook Roberto's shoulder, waking him. He sat up straight. "It's our stop, Roberto," she said.

"Oh. Oh!" he said. Jack, Annie, and Roberto scrambled out of their seats. They jumped off the bus and stood together on the plaza of Metro Insurgentes.

"Do you know how to get to the embassy from here?" Roberto asked.

"Sure. We've been there already," said Annie.

"Good," said Roberto. He shook hands with Annie, then Jack. "Thank you, Annie and

Jack," he said formally. "Thank you for everything."

"Thank *you* for everything, Roberto," said Jack.

"Happy birthday forever," said Annie.

Roberto flashed his beautiful smile. He waved, and then he turned and hurried into the metro station.

"What a great kid," said Jack.

"Yeah, I wish he lived in Frog Creek," said Annie.

"Me too," said Jack. "Well, ready?"

"Yep," said Annie. "Onward to Camelot."

It was dark as Jack and Annie headed up Florencia Avenue. They passed the angel and then ran down the street to the U.S. Embassy.

The embassy grounds were quiet. There was no sign of a guard on duty. "I hope Benny got to see the game on TV," said Annie.

"*I* would like to see that game someday," said Jack. "I'll bet there's a way to see it back home—on the computer, or on a DVD."

"Hey, you really couldn't see anything from Roberto's seat, could you?" said Annie.

Jack shook his head.

"You're a good person, Jack," said Annie.

Before Jack could say he wasn't *that* good, Benny stepped out of the embassy.

"Hi, y'all! Are you just getting back from the game?" he asked.

"Yep," said Jack.

"Did y'all have a good time?" asked Benny.

"Yes!" said Annie.

"And you know what?" said Jack, thinking about running around the soccer field with Annie and Roberto. "It was the game of a lifetime."

"It sure was. I got to see some of it on TV!" said Benny. "I'm headed home now. Night!"

"Good night!" said Annie.

She and Jack stood on the lawn of the embassy until Benny had disappeared down the city sidewalk.

"Pronto," said Annie.

Jack and Annie hurried to the rope ladder hidden in the trees. They climbed up into the magic tree house and looked out the window together.

A fiery waterfall of green-and-yellow stars was bursting above the jagged skyline of Mexico City. With whistling and popping sounds, the fireworks were celebrating the game of a lifetime.

"Good-bye, Mexico," said Jack.

"Good-bye, Pelé!" said Annie.

"Good luck, Roberto!" said Jack.

As the fireworks kept exploding, Jack pulled

out his pencil and notebook, knelt down on the floor, and added the fourth secret of greatness to their list:

ENTHUSIASM

"Good," said Annie. "Let's take our list to Camelot now."

She picked up the scroll lying on the floor and pointed at the word *Camelot* in Merlin's note. "I wish we could go *there*," she whispered.

A blast of light—

a roar of wind—

a rumble of thunder—

and they were *there*.

TEN

Candles in the Forest

Golden light flooded the tree house. Jack and Annie looked out the window. It was early evening. The magic tree house had not landed in a tree. It had landed in a small clearing in a Camelot forest. All around, thousands of lanterns hung from oak trees. Their candle flames shone on knights in gleaming armor and ladies in cone-shaped hats with flowing veils.

Jack couldn't speak. Even Annie was speechless.

Morgan le Fay stepped out from the crowd. The enchantress librarian was dressed in a long red velvet gown. Her white hair shimmered in the candlelight.

"Welcome back, Jack and Annie," said Morgan.

"Thank you," breathed Jack.

"I'm sorry we're so dirty," said Annie. "We just played a tough game of soccer."

"You look wonderful to us," said Morgan, smiling. "All of Camelot celebrates your return. Fifty-two times you have traveled to faraway places in my magic tree house. Fifty-two times you have proven your courage and kindness under the most difficult of circumstances. It is a magical number. The same number as there are weeks in a year."

Carrying his staff, Merlin the magician stepped forward and stood beside Morgan. "Jack and Annie, I heard stories of your adventures long before I met you," he said. "I could not believe two children would venture into the lands of dinosaurs, castles, ancient Egypt, and pirates and return unharmed. You even outsmarted me when you saved Morgan from a spell I had *playfully* put her under."

Morgan gave Merlin a look. Then she turned back to Jack and Annie. "And we had fun, didn't we?" she said. "When we journeyed to the time of the ninjas, the rain forest, the Ice Age, and the moon?"

"Yes, and Jack and I had fun when we solved your four riddles," Annie said breathlessly, "on the coral reef, in the Wild West, on the Serengeti plain of Africa, and in the Arctic."

"And when we became Master Librarians," said Jack, "and rescued the four ancient stories from Rome, China, Ireland, and Greece."

"And when you freed *me* from a spell!" said a voice from the crowd. *"Woof, woof."*

"Teddy!" said Annie.

The firelight shone on the young sorcerer's tousled red hair as he stepped forward. "Remember when I was a dog?" Teddy said, grinning.

Jack and Annie laughed and nodded.

"And we escaped the *Titanic,*" said Teddy, "and the buffalo stampede, the tiger in India, and the forest fire in the Australian outback?"

"Yes!" said Jack and Annie.

"And do not forget how you saved His Majesty from despair," said a woman in a snow-white gown. A veil hung from a wreath of blue flowers around her hair. Standing next to her was a man in a purple tunic and a red cape. On his head was a simple golden crown.

"Queen Guinevere! King Arthur!" said Annie.

"You brought me wisdom and courage from the American Civil War," said King Arthur. "And the Revolutionary War, a schoolhouse on the American prairie, and an earthquake in San Francisco."

"And then you discovered the secrets of everyday magic," said Morgan, "from the people of the first Thanksgiving, the gorillas of the cloud forest, William Shakespeare, and friends in Hawaii."

"And you saved the four treasures of Camelot for Merlin," said King Arthur.

Merlin laughed. "Yes, you outwitted the Dragons of the Otherworld, the Raven King, the Sea Serpent, and the Ice Wizard," he said.

"And do not forget when Teddy and I journeyed with you to the four beautiful cities," said a young girl. Her dark hair curled down over her shoulders. Her sea-blue eyes shone in the firelight. "Ancient Baghdad, Venice, Paris, and New York?" she said.

Jack nodded. "Hi, Kathleen," he said shyly.

"And thank you, Jack and Annie, for saving another from a spell, too," said Kathleen, "on our mission in New York City."

A white unicorn gracefully stepped forward and stood beside Kathleen. He lowered his head.

"Dianthus!" said Annie.

"The Wand of Dianthus helped you learn four secrets of happiness," said Merlin, "from Leonardo da Vinci, Basho the poet, the deep sea— and, best of all, from this little one you brought me from Antarctica." The magician picked up a baby penguin that had been hiding behind his cloak.

"Penny!" said Jack.

"And four creative geniuses of history thank you, too," said Morgan, "for helping them begin the path to giving their gifts to the world."

"Mozart and Louis Armstrong," said Jack, remembering their friends, "and Lady Gregory and Charles Dickens."

"And thank you for helping Teddy to undo the spell he accidentally cast on Penny," said Merlin. "He confessed all to us later."

"We went to the Taj Mahal in India for that," said Annie, "and met Saint Bernard dogs in

Switzerland and Abraham Lincoln—"

"And pandas in China," said Jack.

"And now you have returned from four more missions," said Merlin. "And you were successful, I presume?"

"Yes," said Annie. "We learned secrets of greatness by spending time with Alexander the Great and his black stallion, and with the Great Houdini and his wife, Bess; Florence Nightingale—"

"And finally," said Jack, "from Pelé the Great." He held out the notebook paper on which he had written the four secrets of greatness.

Merlin took the paper from Jack and read in a deep, resonant voice:

HUMILITY

HARD WORK

MEANING AND PURPOSE

ENTHUSIASM

The magician was silent for a moment. He seemed deep in thought. Then he looked back at Jack and Annie. "Yes," he said. "Perfect. Thank you, Jack and Annie, for *your* greatness."

Jack and Annie both smiled and shrugged. "We're not that great," said Jack.

Soccer on Sunday

"We're just two regular kids," said Annie. "Really lucky regular kids."

"On your journeys you have learned many things," said Morgan. "You have seen many parts of the world and met many remarkable people. Jack, you have become kinder and more courageous. Annie, you have become more thoughtful."

"Your next missions may be even more challenging," said Merlin.

"Really?" breathed Jack. "How—how do we prepare for that?"

"Do not worry," said Morgan. "We want you to do what others your age do—learn new things in school, have fun with your family and friends, read books—"

"Play games outside," said Teddy. "Play music."

"Play with animals," added Kathleen.

Jack and Annie smiled.

"Good-bye, Jack and Annie," said Merlin.

"For now," said Morgan.

The candle flames danced wildly in the gentle

breeze. In the golden light, bells rang through the air. Sweet music filled the forest with the sounds of flutes and horns.

The wind began to blow.

The tree house started to spin.

It spun faster and faster.

Then everything was still.

Absolutely still.

⚽ ⚽ ⚽

The pale gold light of dawn shone through the window of the tree house. Jack and Annie were back in the woods of Frog Creek, and their clothes were clean. No time at all had passed in Frog Creek.

"Did—did all that just happen?" said Jack, dazed.

"All what?" said Annie.

"Thousands of candles in the woods, King Arthur and Queen Guinevere, Merlin, Morgan, Teddy, Kathleen, all that?" said Jack.

"I *think*," said Annie.

"Amazing," said Jack. "I wonder what our next mission will be."

"I hope we find out soon," said Annie.

"Yep," said Jack. "Let's go home." He pulled on his backpack and started down the rope ladder. Annie followed him. They stepped onto the ground and started through the summer woods. Neither spoke as they walked under the trees, through patches of shadow and light.

Finally Jack broke the silence. "I think I'll buy a soccer goal with my birthday money," he said. "And set it up in the backyard."

"Good idea," said Annie. "And let's email Jenny and Randy and Quinn and see if they want to practice with us."

"Yeah, and Will and Lallie and Griffin," said Jack. "And I want to pick up some books at the library, too. Check out some exciting ones, with big adventures and interesting information."

"Cool," said Annie.

"Okay, so I guess this is what we'll do today,"

said Jack. "Breakfast, bike to the library and the sports shop, home for lunch, practice soccer, eat dinner, and read before bed."

"Sounds like a good plan," said Annie.

"A perfect one," said Jack.

And they quickened their steps as they left the Frog Creek woods and headed for home.

"Enthusiasm is everything. It must be taut and vibrating like a guitar string."
—Pelé

Author's Note

While working on this book, I had a wonderful time learning about the game of soccer (which is called *football* in other countries). When I was growing up, soccer was not a well-known sport in the United States. In fact, I was hardly aware of soccer until my twenties, when I traveled in Europe and Asia and met many passionate soccer fans.

Of course, since then, soccer has become hugely popular in this country, too—kids everywhere have been asking me to write a book about it.

Once I started researching the subject of soccer, I quickly learned that one of its most important gifts is that it brings people together from all over the world—not only as viewers of the World Cup matches, but as players, too. In countless neighborhoods around the globe, people gather to play the game and simply to have a good time.

Since soccer often brings people together, it should be no surprise that while working on this book, I was brought together with two remarkable people: Kely Nascimento-DeLuca and her son, Malcolm Edson Nascimento DeLuca. They are the daughter and grandson of one of the greatest soccer players of all time—the Brazilian player Edson Arantes do Nascimento, better known as Pelé. I wish I could have met Pelé, too, but he is retired now and lives in Brazil, where he serves as a worldwide ambassador for the game of soccer.

Mary Pope Osborne

Turn the page for a sneak peek at
Magic Tree House Fact Tracker:
Soccer

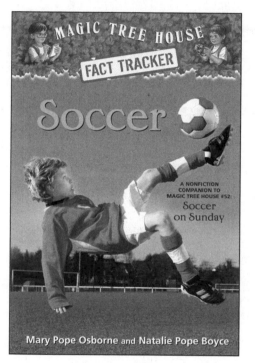

Mia Hamm

Born 1972—United States

Mia was born with a foot problem. As a child, she had an operation and needed a cast and special shoes. Mia's mother says that when she was three, Mia watched some people playing soccer in the park. She ran after the ball and gave it a good kick!

During her career, Mia played in four Women's World Cups. She was also in the 1996, 2000, and 2004 Olympics. Mia was one of the few women ever chosen by FIFA for the list of greatest living players. She's scored 158 goals—that's more goals in international games than anyone except Abby Wambach.

Mia retired after the 2004 Olympics to

raise a family. Because her beloved brother died of a blood disease, Mia began a foundation to help people with similar diseases.

SOAR
– WITH –
READING

A JOINT PROJECT WITH

jetBlue®

MAGIC TREE HOUSE

In 2011, JetBlue launched Soar with Reading, a program designed to help kids' imaginations take flight through reading. Since taking off, JetBlue and its partners have donated over $750,000 worth of books to children.

For more information on how *you* can Soar with Reading, and to find more fun games and activities, please visit:

SoarWithReading.com

1097